To...Our...Sweet...Max.........

with a heart
full of love

Papa + GiGi
2/2017

Love is all around North Carolina

Copyright © 2016 by Sourcebooks, Inc.
Written by Wendi Silvano
Illustrated by Joanna Czernichowska
Design by Quadrum Solutions (www.quadrumltd.com)

Published by Sourcebooks Jabberwocky, an imprint of Sourcebooks, Inc.
P.O. Box 4410, Naperville, Illinois 60567-4410
(630) 961-3900
Fax: (630) 961-2168
www.sourcebooks.com

Source of Production: Worzalla, Stevens Point, Wisconsin
Date of Production: November 2016
Run Number: 5008153
Printed and bound in the United States of America.
WOZ 10 9 8 7 6 5 4 3

Love is all around North Carolina

Written by Wendi Silvano

Illustrated by Joanna Czernichowska

sourcebooks
jabberwocky

Love is a feeling that comes from **inside.**

Everyone feels it. It can't be denied.

But how do we know that it's there? What's the clue?

How can we **see** it?

Just what can we do?

Love's all around, if you just pay attention,

in people and places too many to mention.

Go look at the **park,**

on the **street,**

at the **mall.**

You'll see love all over. It's **big** and it's small!

In North Carolina, in cars and on trains,
in taxis and buses, on boats and on planes,
in Charlotte, and Durham,
and Fayetteville too,
you'll find there is love that will come into view.

Cape Fear River

Right there, on the lawn, in North Cary Park

is a mom with her babe,

hearing songs of a lark.

She **swaddles** him, **cuddles** him,
kisses his ear.

That surely is **love**,
it's perfectly clear!

At a store up in **Asheville,** a girl gets a bear.
She **squeezes** him,
squishes him,
ruffles his hair.

It's clear that she **loves** him. She's **smiling** and bright.

She tucks him in **softly** and **gently** at night.

That same little girl, the very next day,
sees a **friend** at her school who is too **sad** to play.

So she sits down beside him and **listens** and **shares,**
making sure that he knows there's someone who **cares.**

Now the boy who was **sad** feels much **better**, you see,

so he runs home all happy to play with **Magee.**

They **romp** and they **frolic.**

They **fetch** and they **run.**

It's certain he **loves** him. They're having such **fun!**

You can see how **love** travels

when **shared** with a friend.

If *everyone* shares love, it never will end.

From one to another, it s p r e a d s and it **grows**.

You can't have *too much*, as everyone knows.

An officer in Raleigh who **helps** change a flat.

A fireman in Mooresville who **rescues** a cat.

BANK OF AMERICA STADIUM

The home team that makes the crowd **cheer** and **clap.**
Each moment has **love** like a **gift** you unwrap.

There's a **father** who sits at the table each night,
helping out with the homework to get it just **right**.
He's tired and busy, but that's **love**, you know…
giving up what you want to **help** someone else **grow**.

It's not only *people* who show love, it's true.

Just come see the creatures

that play at the zoo!

The polar bear tumbles

and rolls with her cub,

and when they are finished,

she gives him a rub.

Where else is there **love?** Have we looked all around?

I think we've forgotten—love grows from the ground!

In the **meadows** and **gardens** and parks you will find

that the earth shows us **love** of all shapes and all kinds.

Wherever you look, love comes into sight.

It's there in the morning, it's there in the night.

But in North Carolina,

the best love you'll find

is a love that is gentle,

and selfless, and kind...

It's the love found at home. It shows up each day
in things people do and in things people say.
There's no greater love, I can tell you, it's true,
than the love of your family...

Especially for YOU!